Dear Parents:

Congratulations! Your child is taking the first steps on an exciting journey. The destination? Independent reading!

STEP INTO READING® will help your child get there. The program offers five steps to reading success. Each step includes fun stories and colorful art or photographs. In addition to original fiction and books with favorite characters, there are Step into Reading Non-Fiction Readers, Phonics Readers and Boxed Sets, Sticker Readers, and Comic Readers—a complete literacy program with something to interest every child.

Learning to Read, Step by Step!

Ready to Read Preschool–Kindergarten
• big type and easy words • rhyme and rhythm • picture clues
For children who know the alphabet and are eager to begin reading.

Reading with Help Preschool–Grade 1
• basic vocabulary • short sentences • simple stories
For children who recognize familiar words and sound out new words with help.

Reading on Your Own Grades 1–3
• engaging characters • easy-to-follow plots • popular topics
For children who are ready to read on their own.

Reading Paragraphs Grades 2–3
• challenging vocabulary • short paragraphs • exciting stories
For newly independent readers who read simple sentences with confidence.

Ready for Chapters Grades 2–4
• chapters • longer paragraphs • full-color art
For children who want to take the plunge into chapter books but still like colorful pictures.

STEP INTO READING® is designed to give every child a successful reading experience. The grade levels are only guides; children will progress through the steps at their own speed, developing confidence in their reading.

Remember, a lifetime love of reading starts with a single step!

Step into Reading, Random House, and the Random House colophon are registered trademarks
of Penguin Random House LLC.

Visit us on the Web!
StepIntoReading.com
randomhousekids.com

Educators and librarians, for a variety of teaching tools, visit us at RHTeachersLibrarians.com

ISBN 978-0-7364-3588-8 (trade) — ISBN 978-0-7364-8180-9 (lib. bdg.)
ISBN 978-0-7364-3589-5 (ebook)

Printed in the United States of America
10 9 8 7 6 5 4 3 2 1

DISNEY

FROZEN

NORTHERN LIGHTS

THE RIGHT TRACK

adapted by Apple Jordan

based on the original story
by Suzanne Francis

illustrated by the
Disney Storybook Art Team

Random House 🏠 New York

Kristoff and his friends
are going
to Troll Valley.

Tomorrow is
the Crystal Ceremony.
They will help
the trolls celebrate!

A troll named Little Rock
greets them.

Little Rock is sad.
His tracking crystal
will not glow.
He cannot be
in the ceremony
if he is not
a good tracker.

Grand Pabbie is gone!

"Let's track him,"

says Kristoff.

Little Rock agrees.

He will find Grand Pabbie
and make his
tracking crystal glow!

The friends set off
on their journey.
Little Rock
leads the way.

Little Rock picks

up a scent.

He thinks it is

Grand Pabbie!

But it is only Sven.

The friends climb
a large mountain.
Anna and Elsa
tell stories.

They help Little Rock

feel brave.

Soon they come
to a frozen river.

They try to cross.

The ice cracks!

Little Rock almost
falls in.
Kristoff and Anna
help him.

Elsa waves her arms.
She makes a stairway
of ice.

It stretches
across the river.

Little Rock and Olaf
run down the steps.
The steps begin
to fall.

Elsa uses her magic.

She makes ice sleds.

The friends jump on.
They race across
the frozen river.

Little Rock thanks his
friends for saving him.
He shares a crystal
with Anna and Elsa.

They know Little Rock
will soon light
his tracking crystal, too . . .

. . . even if he needs
a little help
from his friends!